To my new nephew, Dylan Louie.
Another one of the world's cutest creatures.

WALKER BOOKS
AND SUBSIDIARIES
LONDON • BOSTON • SYDNEY

What Is Mr. Winkle?

Lara Jo Regan

What is Mr. Winkle?

Mr. Winkle entered my life in a manner as improbable and mystical as he is. Lost in an industrial area on my way home from a photography assignment, I spotted an odd tuft of fluff on the side of the road. Moving close enough to take in its diminutive dimensions and enormous, other-worldly eyes, I thought it might be a shipwrecked alien. In the glow of the headlights, this muddy, tattered little creature hobbled straight into my arms, as if he'd been waiting for me all along.

After a year of vet visits and tender loving care, my peculiar pint-sized pal was well enough to lead a normal life. It took even longer to come up with a name worthy of his uniqueness. Finally, it came to me – Mr. Winkle! Of course.

As his health improved, Mr. Winkle began to meet people on his daily walks, all of whom offered theories as to his identity. "It's a robotic squirrel!" screamed a cable repairman. "It's a cat in a dog suit," surmised an out-of-work actor. "He's a furry smile!" exclaimed a Japanese tourist.

It was these hilarious, inspired reactions from mesmerized strangers that sparked the idea for the *What Is Mr. Winkle?* photo series. His power to heal, enchant and entertain was too overwhelming to keep to myself. I simply had to share him with the world through my photography. Mr. Winkle made it easy, supermodel that he turned out to be. He loves the camera, hamming it up with all his heart, as if he knows it's his mission to make us happy.

What is Mr. Winkle? Well, that's for you to decide. I'm sure you will choose a favourite character or two. Mine is one I haven't made a photo of yet, but I think it may be what Mr. Winkle *truly* is: the child of a cloud, on loan from heaven.

– Lara Jo Regan

A Ghost?

A Bumblebear?

A Thirsty Camel?

An Ancient Koala?

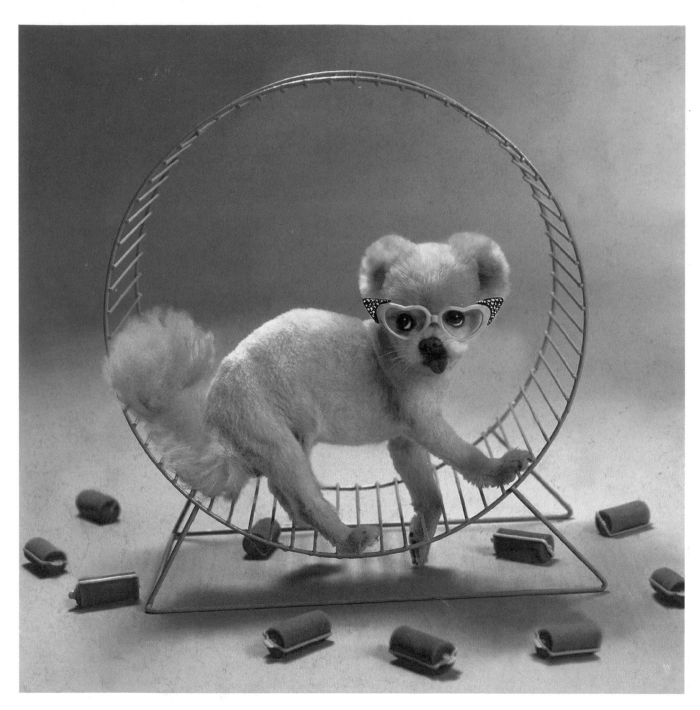

A Hamster with a Perm?

Perry Winkle?

A Japanese Cartoon Character?

A BEDROOM SLIPPER?

a stuffed Animal?

A Cat in a Dog Suit?

A Furry Buddha?

A Marionette?

A Wood Sprite?

A Bowwow Ballerina?

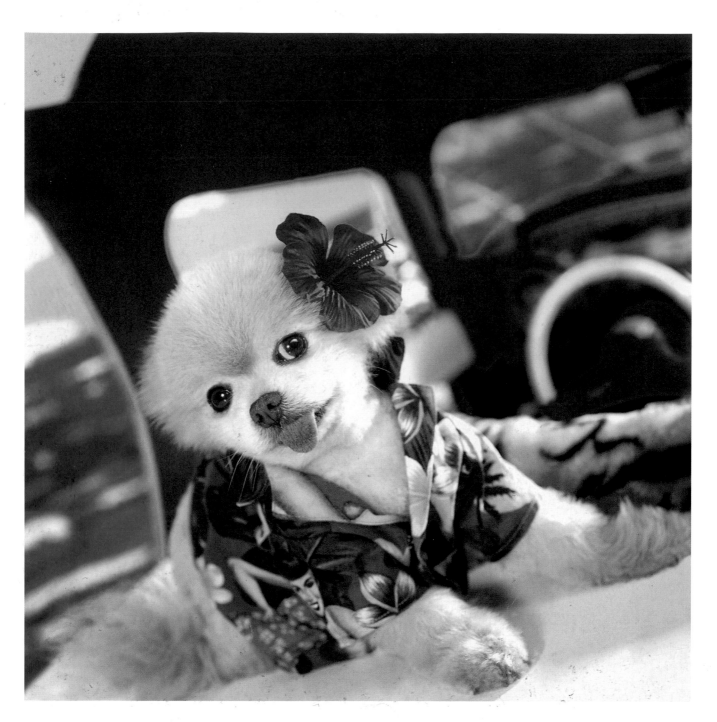

A Dashboard Ornament?

A LABORATORY CREATION?

AN ALIEN?

A HALLUCINATION?

A Devil?

An Angel?

What *Is* Mr. Winkle?

The cutest dog in the universe!

(A Pom-pom?)

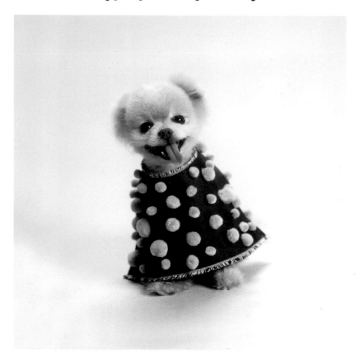

First published in Great Britain 2004 by Walker Books Ltd
87 Vauxhall Walk, London SE11 5HJ

2 4 6 8 10 9 7 5 3 1

Copyright © 2001 Lara Jo Regan
Photographs © 2001, 2002 Lara Jo Regan

Published by arrangement with Random House Children's Books, a division of Random House, Inc., New York, USA

Printed in Singapore

British Library Cataloguing in Publication Data:
a catalogue record for this book is available from the British Library

ISBN 1-84428-015-2

www.walkerbooks.co.uk